A YARN OF MURDER

HOMESPUN CROCHET COZY MYSTERIES, BOOK 1

PATTI BENNING

SUMMER PRESCOTT BOOKS PUBLISHING

Copyright 2021 Summer Prescott Books

All Rights Reserved. No part of this publication nor any of the information herein may be quoted from, nor reproduced, in any form, including but not limited to: printing, scanning, photocopying, or any other printed, digital, or audio formats, without prior express written consent of the copyright holder.

**This book is a work of fiction. Any similarities to persons, living or dead, places of business, or situations past or present, is completely unintentional.

CHAPTER ONE

Josephina Thompson gazed out her kitchen window as she washed the dishes left over from lunch. The window looked out over her long, dirt driveway. A big, red barn was just visible on the right, and on either side of the drive were wooden fences that used to be white. Over the years the paint had cracked and peeled until the natural wood of the planks showed through, leaving only a few flakes of white paint here and there.

Inside the fences were alpacas, and it was one of these that she was currently watching. To the left of the driveway, one of her male alpacas — also called "machos" — named Darwin, was doing his best to cause trouble. He had a beautiful, freshly shorn, red coat, and was currently working at the gate latch with his lips, his long neck crimped awkwardly over the top railing.

She was almost certain she had remembered to engage the padlock after she fed them this morning, but there was always a chance it had slipped her mind. Most of her alpacas were happy to spend their days grazing, lounging in the shade, or playing together, but Darwin was an escape artist. She had no doubt that if he managed to get the gate open, he would make a beeline across the driveway to the opposite pasture, where her female alpacas — also called "hembras" — were. Since females would often spit at males if they weren't in the mood to be bothered, it had the potential to be a messy, if entertaining, incident.

"Jo!"

She jumped at the sound of her name being shouted only feet away from her and nearly dropped the plate she was washing in the sink. Turning, she saw her boyfriend, Cole Knight, watching her with a mix of irritation and amusement.

"Sorry," she said, shutting off the water. "Did you say something?"

He heaved out a sigh. "I called your name twice and you didn't even blink. I have to get going. I'm showing a house in half an hour. Are we still on for tonight?"

"Definitely," she replied with a smile, pausing to dry her hands before moving over to give him a quick kiss. He barely paused to give her a distracted peck on the lips before continuing.

"Right, well, last time you canceled five minutes before we were supposed to meet, so I want to be sure. I'm not driving all the way out to Port Austin if you're just going to leave me hanging again."

"I canceled last time because I had to have the vet out to see to Marcy," she said, stung. Marcy was her first alpaca that was getting up there in age at sixteen. She had been spending an unusual amount of time lying down the week before and had refused to stand up when Jo went out to check on her, so Jo had wanted to make sure nothing was wrong with her. "I'll be there tonight, I promise."

"All right," he said, already turning to grab his satchel. "Have a good day."

"You, too."

She watched from the front porch as he left, feeling inordinately sad. Cole had been more and more irritated lately, and she didn't know if it was because of her or his work. He was a real-estate agent and hadn't had many sales in the last couple of months. With luck, the house he was showing today would get sold quickly, and he would start getting back to his old, cheerful self.

The rattle of a gate made her glance over at Darwin, who was still working on the latch. With a sigh, she went back inside to shove her feet into a pair of rubber boots, then marched across the gravel driveway to check on the padlock. Sure enough, the chain she used to secure the gate was locked shut, and unless Darwin had learned to use a key since yesterday, he was secure in the pasture.

"What are you doing, you silly boy?" she asked, ruffling his topknot, the portion of longer fleece on his head that she left when shearing the alpacas.

Her two other males, a black alpaca named Coal — she had bought him before she met Cole, or she would have named him something else to avoid confusion — and a white one named Yeti, came trotting over to shove their heads over the fence as well. She patted each of them in turn, their big eyes and soft hair bringing a smile back to her face. The alpacas were not only the cornerstone of her business but were also a major source of joy in the rest of her life. They were such gentle, goofy creatures, and never failed to cheer her up.

"No more escape attempts, all right, Darwin?" she asked, giving him an extra scratch between the ears. "Today's a busy day, and I don't have time to go chasing you all over creation. If you absolutely must get out, at least wait until tomorrow. Deal?"

The sound of tires on gravel forced her attention away from the alpacas, but it was just someone driving down her neighbor's driveway. She owned nearly thirty acres, but it was a narrow strip of land, longer than it was wide, and her closest neighbor, a lovely older woman named Rose Cantrell, was right on the other side of the male alpacas' pasture. She waved, recognizing the truck that was leaving as belonging to the man who lived on the other side of Rose's property, Dale Fisher. The truck slowed as he honked in greeting. The sound made the alpacas flinch, and she crooned to them as he went on his way.

Once all of the males, including Darwin, had returned to nibbling at the hay she had left for them earlier that morning, she turned around and marched back across the driveway to say hello to her girls. She had six female alpacas in all, two of which had big round bellies and were due to give birth at any time. Alpacas had a gestation period that lasted nearly twelve months, so these babies, or crias, were long-awaited. She clucked her tongue and watched all of the girls begin making their way over to her. She had spent a lot of time working with the alpacas to make sure they were all as friendly as they were. It was to their benefit if they enjoyed interacting with people; it made the necessary shearing, handling, and vet checks much less stressful to them.

She greeted each of the girls by name, spending extra time on Marcy, who had been slowing down lately. She was another white alpaca, though her white wasn't as bright as Yeti's was, anymore. Too old to breed but still the matriarch of the herd, Marcy had more than earned her retirement here, and Jo wanted to do everything she could to make sure the old girl's final years were full of comfort and peace.

"You girls don't cause any trouble, do you? No, you're such good girls." She continued on, talking to each of them in turn, before finally turning to go back into her house, sidestepping a chicken that was scratching at the ground right behind her reflexively, her mind already on the chores she would have to get done in the coming days and weeks.

The alpacas would need to be moved to new pastures soon, since their grass was getting a bit scarce, but she was really hoping that the two hembras who were due any day would give birth before that happened, since she wanted them closer to the house in case anything went wrong. She would also need to clean the chicken coop out, and she needed to do some fence repairs and look into buying some sheep, which she had been meaning to do for years… the list was never ending, and that was just what she needed to do to take care of the animals. She had bags upon bags of alpaca fleece to spin into yarn, as well as the sheep wool, goat hair, and even some dog fur that she needed to spin both for clients and for sale at her yarn shop.

She also had to make time for her friends and neighbors. Speaking of which, she had to get going over to Rose's soon. She had a skein of yarn made from Yeti's white fleece and dyed a beautiful maroon that she was going to gift to her neighbor in exchange for a pair of pies, and a slice of pie was sounding pretty good right about now. She and Cole had just eaten lunch together, but they had skipped dessert, which was simply a travesty.

Humming to herself, she stepped inside and pulled her boots off, shutting the door on the farm and the heat before going into her spinning room to find the skein she wanted to give to Rose.

CHAPTER TWO

Jo knocked on Rose's door, taking in a deep breath at the delicious scent of freshly baked pies that was wafting out of an open window. The door opened, and she came face to face with a pretty young woman, her light brown hair pulled back into a ponytail, not a strand out of place. Jo's own auburn hair was in a messy bun, and for a moment she wished she had taken more time to pretty herself up before Cole came over that morning.

"Hi, Harper," she said. "I'm here to see Rose, if she's got a few minutes."

"Of course," Harper replied with a smile. She stepped back and gestured Jo inside. "She mentioned something about you stopping by. Are you the reason she won't let me have a slice of pie?"

Jo grinned. "Probably. But if you tell me she's starving you, I won't believe it."

Harper laughed. "You're right. She didn't let me have any pie, but she did make a batch of lemon poppy seed muffins for breakfast. I may have had one… or three."

Rose was a retired widow, who spent most of her time baking. Harper, her great-niece, benefited from her love of baked goods whenever she came by to help out, and Rose and Jo had long since agreed to a trade system, skeins of yarn in exchange for more baked goods than she could eat on her own. It was a deal that left everyone happy, and just one of the things that Jo loved about living in such a close-knit community. The small town of Flatstone, Michigan, was located in the state's thumb area and only half an hour's drive from Lake Huron, one of the four great lakes that the state was known for. Outwardly, it was a tiny farming community that didn't seem to have much going for it, but to Jo it was paradise. She had grown up there and knew the area and the people like the back of her hand. Nowhere else had ever given her such a feeling of community, and if there was one thing Jo needed, it was a sense of belonging.

She found Rose in the kitchen, knitting something at the table. Her white hair was thin, but perfectly styled into curls that bounced when she looked up. "Jo, there you are. I thought you'd be over earlier. Your pies are on the counter, one blueberry and one rhubarb, just liked you asked for."

"They smell wonderful," Jo said. "I can't wait to try them. And, sorry about that. Cole and I had lunch together and it took a little bit longer than I thought it would. Here's that yarn, made from Yeti's fleece, just like you wanted." She put the bag containing the skein of yarn on the table.

"Don't you worry about it. I was just concerned that your pies wouldn't be warm anymore by the time you got here. You will sit and have a piece with me, won't you? If that boyfriend of yours is still around, you should call him over, too. He stopped by on his way to your place with some fresh eggs, and I put aside a few muffins for him as thanks."

"He had to leave a little while ago for a showing, but I can take the muffins for him, if you'd like. And yes, I'd love to sit with you for a few minutes. I've got to get to work soon, but I can always spare the time for pie and good company."

"Wonderful." Rose's wrinkled face split into a smile. "Harper, can you get plates out for all of us?" She pulled the bag containing the yarn toward her and removed the skein, stroking the soft yarn with her fingers. "This is just lovely, Jo. The color is so rich, and it's so soft. I suppose I can forgive that alpaca of yours for spitting on me, if this is what I get out of it. He really does produce lovely fleece."

Jo grinned as she sat down. Earlier that year, Darwin had gotten out of the pasture and made his way into Rose's yard. Rose had gone out to try to herd him back onto Jo's property and had gotten in the middle of a spitting spat between him and Yeti, who had taken exception to Darwin's prancing around on the other side of the fence. Alpacas rarely spat at humans, and Jo didn't think Yeti had been aiming at Rose but getting hit with a spray of partially digested grass and hay couldn't have been fun, either way. Rose had, only half-jokingly, said that Yeti owed her a sweater, which was why she wanted the next skein Jo gave her to be made from his fleece.

Harper got three plates and three forks out and set them down on the table, then glanced at Jo. "Which pie do you want a piece of?"

"I'm in a blueberry mood," Jo said. "But feel free to cut yourself a piece of either."

It wasn't long before each of them had a piece of still-warm pie on their plates. Harper hovered behind her chair, making sure they all had everything they needed. "Can I get you anything, Aunt Rose? Maybe some of that lemonade you made this morning? Jo?"

"I'm good with water, thanks," Jo replied. "I can get it myself, Harper. You don't have to get it for me."

"I'll have water, too," Rose said. "Andrea's coming over later, and I want to save the lemonade for our lunch."

Harper waved off Jo's offer to get the water herself and poured a glass for each of them, before finally sitting down. Jo knew she had been helping her Aunt Rose for years now, ever since Rose's husband died, but only recently had she started getting paid for her work, along with being offered increased hours. Rose had told Jo in private that Harper had quit her job to help her, and she wanted to help her great-niece make ends meet. It was a situation that benefitted both of them. Rose could still get around pretty well, but she was definitely slowing down, and a set of helping hands was likely invaluable to her.

The pie was delicious, which came as no surprise to Jo, and she finished her piece quickly. She was tempted to try a slice of the rhubarb, too, but she had to be at the yarn shop in just half an hour. The second pie would have to wait until after dinner.

Ignoring Harper's protest that she would take care of the dishes, Jo carried her plate and fork to the sink and washed them. When she went to throw her napkin away, she spotted an empty container of eyedrops on the floor and scooped it up to throw away as well, then said her goodbyes. With a reminder from Rose, and a promise to pass them on to Cole, she wrapped up a pair of lemon poppy seed muffins before leaving. Carrying both pie plates and the muffins back over to her own house took some balancing, but she managed. With one last look at the rhubarb pie, now sitting covered on her counter, and a mental promise to come back for it later, she hurried into her spinning room to gather her things for work.

CHAPTER THREE

"Please tell me you have a pair of adorable baby alpacas prancing around in the fields at your house."

Jo smiled as she placed the balls of yarn in a paper bag. Laurie Mesick was a longtime client and a good friend of hers, and while she wasn't a fan of some of the messier aspects of farm life, she adored Jo's alpacas.

"Not yet, but they should be coming any day now," she replied. "I promise I'll take pictures as soon as they're born."

"You have to invite me over once they are. I bet they're going to be just adorable."

Jo grinned as she handed over the bag. "My teenage

self would have been horrified to hear me say this, but baby alpacas are even cuter than puppies."

They chatted for a few more minutes until Laurie said goodbye, leaving the shop with her purchases tucked under her arm. Jo gave a contented sigh and leaned back in the tall chair behind the register. It had been a busy day — well, a busy day for the yarn shop — and she was looking forward to getting home and taking a short break before getting ready to meet Cole for dinner. The shop closed at five every day, which gave her plenty of free time in the evenings. With an eye on the minute hand of a nearby clock as it edged past five, she stood up and began counting out the register. Even though she accepted credit cards, a good number of her customers tended to pay in cash. Full Skein Ahead served people of all ages and backgrounds, but she couldn't deny that a big chunk of her customers were on the older side of the spectrum. That was gradually changing, though; knitting and crocheting had both become a bit more popular with the younger crowd, lately. It wasn't just a hobby for the elderly. There was a lot to be said for being able to make your own clothing and accessories, and Jo had hosted a few crocheting and knitting classes over the years that had been met with quite a bit of success.

She also had a few younger people in her crochet club. Her youngest was sixteen. The girl had started attending with her mother, but when her mother's work hours changed, she kept coming on her own. She made gorgeous shawls, and Jo intended to talk to her about selling some of them in the yarn shop – with her mother's approval, of course.

The yarn shop wasn't her only source of income. As much as she loved it, she would never get rich off of it. She also sold spun alpaca fleece online and got paid to spin various fibers for clients around the country. She also sold the occasional alpaca, usually only the males. They could be a bit troublesome, more so than the females, so she didn't want to have more than three of them. Darwin alone was more trouble than the entire rest of the herd.

On top of the yarn, she also sold homemade knitted and crocheted items in the store. She worked with a couple of local craftsmen and women who got a cut of the profits when one of their items sold. It was a small boost to her income, but the price handmade items sold for could never compensate for the sheer number of man-hours that went into making something like a sweater.

As it was, she usually made just enough to cover all of her expenses and put a little bit away in savings each year. She wouldn't be able to retire for a long, long while, but she didn't mind. She was happy with what she did. In fact, she was happy with almost everything in her life. She had a good boyfriend, even with the rough patch they were going through right now, and she and her lovely alpacas had a beautiful home on plenty of land. She had a business that she loved, good friends, and couldn't think of a better town in which to spend her life.

When she was done with the register, she moved around the small store to straighten the few skeins and balls of yarn that had gotten misplaced throughout the day. Kaylee, one of two employees who worked for her part-time, had done a good job straightening up before her shift ended, so there wasn't much left to do. She didn't make all of the yarn that she sold, but all of it, other than the small section of synthetic fibers, were made locally. She had partnerships with a couple of different farms throughout the area, and offered both sheep and alpaca yarn along with a small selection of specialty yarns that varied depending on what sort of fur, fleece, or hair she got in. She sold everything from cashmere yarn to yarn made from fluffy dog fur.

Satisfied that the yarn shop was ready for opening the next morning, Jo gathered her things and stepped outside, locking the door behind her. It was still sunny out, and she took a moment to simply bask in the light before turning toward her car, a slightly beat up dark blue crossover. The yarn shop was a block away from the main street that ran through the center of Flatstone in a quiet, semi-residential area. The building itself was an old house, the bottom of which Jo leased from the owner, who lived upstairs. She rarely saw her landlady, since the older woman traveled frequently, but when she did, they always stopped to chat for little while. Jo had been leasing space from her for nearly eight years now and hoped that their arrangement wouldn't end anytime soon. She had grown to love the place and didn't want to have to deal with the hassle of finding a new building to lease. She didn't want the commitment that came with purchasing space. For the past couple of years, she had been playing around with the idea of building a small shop on her own property, which would be costly at first but would hopefully save money in the long run. As an added bonus, her customers would get to see the alpacas where the majority of her yarn came from in person.

Her mind filled with possibilities for the future, she hit the button on her keys to unlock her car and slipped into the driver's seat, taking her time to arrange her things and make sure the radio was tuned to her favorite station to listen to in the evenings.

Before she could pull away from the curb, a cheerful tune sounded in the car as her phone started ringing. She glanced at it, spotted Rose's name on the caller ID, and quickly answered. As her neighbor, Rose was usually the first one to call if something was wrong at the farm. Jo's mind immediately flashed to visions of predator attacks, fires, or escaped alpacas. Fearing the worst, she answered with a shaky voice. "Rose? Is everything all right?"

"Sorry for interrupting your day, Jo," her friend said. "Nothing's wrong, you don't have to worry about that, I was just wondering if you could do me a quick favor."

Feeling an immediate rush of relief, Jo relaxed against the seat. "Of course. What can I do for you?"

"Harper took me out to do some shopping. When I left, Andrea was still there. She was looking through some of my old things to see if there was anything that her grandchildren might want. I asked her to lock up when she leaves, but I forgot to tell her where the spare key was, and now she's not answering her phone. I'm worried that the house may be sitting there unlocked. I know the chances of anything happening are low, but I'd really appreciate it if you could help me out and make sure it's locked up when you get home."

"I'm just getting out of work, so I'll be home in a couple of minutes. I can swing by and make sure it's locked up. I'll give you a call afterward, so you'll know it's done."

"Thanks, Jo. I think I owe you another pie."

Jo smiled despite herself. "Really, it's no problem, Rose. That's what neighbors are for, after all. If we don't stick together, then who will?"

They said their goodbyes and Jo ended the call. She replaced her phone and then put the car into drive, pulling out along the curb and turning at the end of the block. She decided to stop by Rose's house first. It would be faster than walking over after she got home, and she really wanted some time to relax before she got ready to go meet Cole at the restaurant in Port Austin.

As she pulled up Rose's driveway, she glanced over at the pasture between their houses to make sure Darwin hadn't managed to manufacture an escape while she was gone. The sight of all three of the male alpacas relaxing in the shade of their lean-to made her smile. They might be trouble sometimes, but they made up for it by being absolutely adorable.

She turned her attention back to Rose's house and frowned. There was a red car sitting in the driveway that she hadn't noticed when she first pulled off the road. She wasn't sure, but she thought it was Andrea's. Andrea was someone she only knew in passing; she was in her mid-fifties and was a close friend to the much older Rose. She was a local but didn't participate in any of the same groups or activities that Jo did. She knew through the grapevine that Andrea was recently divorced but didn't know the details — and hadn't asked. If there was one thing she disliked about living in such a small town, it was the way rumors and gossip spread like wildfire. She was guilty of it herself occasionally, but she did her best to let people keep their own business to themselves if they wanted to.

After pulling to a halt beside the car, she got out and made her way up to the porch, looking around in case the visitor was outside somewhere. The front door was shut but opened easily when she turned the handle.

"Hello?" she called out, hesitating before crossing the threshold. She didn't want to take Rose's visitor by surprise, but she owed it to her neighbor to see what was going on. From the sound of what Rose had said on the phone, Andrea should have left by now.

It wasn't the first time she had been in Rose's house alone, but as she stepped through the front door, the house seemed strangely silent, as if it was holding its breath. The air conditioning was on full blast, and she shut the front door behind her so as not to waste the cold air.

"Is anyone here?" she called out. "It's Jo, from next door. Rose asked me to stop by and make sure the door was locked."

There was no response, no sound at all, except for the gentle hum of the air conditioner. Feeling uneasy, even though she couldn't quite put her finger on why, she continued moving through the house, looking around to see if anything was out of place. The house seemed just as it was when she left that morning, except for the kitchen. She stepped inside, her eyes on the cardboard boxes on the round kitchen table. They were all open, and there was a pile of clothes and old children's toys sitting on the table, as if someone had been going through them. Rose had said Andrea was looking through some of her old things to see if her grandchildren might want anything. Jo was a bit surprised that the other woman had left such a mess, and felt her lips pulling into a frown as she turned to head back outside.

That was when she saw the legs sticking out from the other side of the island. She felt as if someone had doused her in a tub of cold water and froze for a long moment before taking a hesitant step forward.

"Hello? Are you okay?"

There was no response. Cautiously, she edged along the counter and around the island, gasping when she saw the full scene unfold in front of her. The person lying on the floor was Andrea. Jo had lived on a farm long enough to recognize when something was dead, and there was no question that Andrea had taken her last breath some time ago. Her body was unmarked, and her hair spread in a halo around her head. On top of the island was a pitcher of lemonade and a spilled glass, as if she had been in the middle of pouring herself more when she collapsed.

Jo pressed both hands to her mouth and took a step back. She blinked, squeezing her eyes shut tightly and opening them again, as if that would change things, but the scene in front of her remained the same. Taking a shaky breath, she turned, and half ran toward the door. She had left her phone in the car. This wouldn't be the first time she'd had to call 911 for someone, but she really hoped it would be the last.

CHAPTER FOUR

"And you're not a resident of this house?"

Jo bit back a sigh. The police kept asking her questions that seemed horribly unimportant to her. She just wanted them to get to the meat of things, figuring out what happened to Andrea.

"That's right. Like I said, I'm Rose's neighbor. I live right over there." She pointed at her own house, which was maybe two hundred yards away, on the other side of the pasture where Darwin and the other alpacas were staring at the flashing lights of the police vehicles over the fence.

"And why were you inside the house?"

"Rose called me to ask if I would check her door to

make sure it was locked. She had let Andrea stay here alone earlier to look through some boxes of things for her grandchildren."

"Did your neighbor… Rose… say why she didn't stay with her?"

"I don't know," Jo said. "I'm guessing she had errands she wanted to get done but didn't want to hurry Andrea. They were close friends. Rose doesn't drive, so she can only go into town when her niece, Harper, is able to drive her."

"I see." He made a note, and Jo tried not to let her curiosity show on her face. She didn't watch much TV, but she did read a lot of books, and she knew that police weren't in the habit of sharing too much with anyone outside of the investigation. "Can you tell me more about your personal relationship with the deceased?"

She wasn't sure how that would help but nodded and began telling him about the few times she and Andrea had both been over at Rose's house at the same time. At least he was being very thorough. She wasn't sure what to think about Andrea's death, but the fact that Rose and by extension, she, would have an answer soon helped to soothe the horrible mix of curiosity and horror that had been battling in her ever since she found the body.

The sun was beginning to dip in the sky by the time she was free to return to her house. She made the short drive, parked in her usual spot between the house and the pasture where the female alpacas stayed, glanced out the driver's side window, and let out a yelp of surprise.

Scrabbling with her seatbelt, she threw the driver's door open and hurried over to the fence, her eyes widening as she gazed at a tiny bundle of fawn colored fur lying with its legs tucked under it on the soft grass. The cria's mother stood over it, occasionally lowering her head to nuzzle the baby's fur. A quick look around the field showed her that the other pregnant hembra hadn't given birth yet, but one out of two wasn't bad. She opened the gate and stepped inside, making cooing noises as she approached the pair. The mother extended her neck, her nostrils flaring as she sniffed at Jo inquisitively, then she seemed to relax and went back to eating grass next to her baby.

All of her feelings about what happened to Andrea got pushed to the side for the time being. Jo knelt on the grass next to the new baby and carefully extended a hand to stroke its soft fur. A quick check showed that the baby was a female, which meant that she would be staying here, likely for the rest of her life.

"You're just so perfect," Jo whispered as she pet the baby alpaca. She guessed that the mother had given birth a few hours ago, since the cria's fur was dry. As she watched, the baby stood on shaky legs and tottered over to its mother.

Jo sat back on her heels, unable to help the grin that spread across her face as she watched the pair. *I'll have to think of the perfect name,* she thought. She had a list, somewhere, but none of them seemed right for this newest addition.

After watching them for a few more minutes, she decided to go in and get some work done. The cria wouldn't pay for its first checkup with the vet by being cute, after all. Making sure she locked the gate behind her, she went back to her car to get her things before heading into the house. The police were still over at Rose's house; her friend had returned a short while ago and was talking with them as they tried to figure out what had happened. Jo had heard the words "heart attack" mentioned before she left and wondered if it was as simple as that. She didn't know enough about Andrea to know if she had any health issues, but she supposed it made sense. She didn't know what else could have possibly hurt the other woman in the safety of Rose's kitchen.

Propping the window open so she could hear if the alpacas started crying out – she was always especially worried about predators after a recent birth – she grabbed a bag of fleece that she was supposed to turn into a ball of yarn for a client and settled down on the comfortable chair in her spinning room. The air was gradually cooling off outside, and the sounds of nature that came in through the open window comforted her. Finding Andrea had been horrible, but the more she thought about it, the more she was glad that she had been the one to do it rather than Rose. Rose was quite healthy for her age, but Jo didn't want to think about what the shock of finding her friend dead on her kitchen floor would do to her.

Jo lost herself in her work for the next hour, the time slipping by as she slowly processed the fleece. Normally, she would listen to an audiobook or the radio while doing this, but she wanted to be able to hear the alpacas in case something went wrong.

When a sound eventually did force her out of her concentration, it was not the sound of panicked alpacas but the sound of tires on gravel.

She blinked, set aside the fleece she was working on, and rose out of her chair. She didn't get very many unannounced visitors all the way out here, and her first thought was that it was the police, coming back to ask her even more questions.

As soon as she stepped out on the front porch, she saw that she was wrong. Even in the dark, she could tell that it wasn't a vehicle she recognized. It was a pickup truck, one of the newer models, and was dark gray or black. The driver parked next to her car and shut off the engine. She stood on her porch, her arms crossed as she waited to see who it was.

The driver's side door opened and shut with a slam and the driver began walking up toward the porch. She could tell it was a man, but she couldn't see much else until he stepped into the ring of porch light.

"Nick?" she gasped when the light finally revealed his face. It had been over fifteen years since she had last seen him, but even though the skin around his eyes was more lined now, and the dark bristles of a few days' growth of beard on his chin was thicker, he didn't look all that much different at thirty-five than he had at eighteen. He had filled out some, but he had always been well-built, since he had grown up working with his father at the family's machine shop.

He grinned at her, and it was the same grin that she remembered from their high school years together, slightly crooked, but with white, straight teeth. "Hey, Jo. Mary West down at the grocery store said that you still lived out here. I was sorry to hear about your parents."

"It happened ten years ago," she said. "I'm sorry about it, too, but I've come to terms with it. What in the world are you doing back here, Nicholas Moore? This is like seeing a ghost." She'd already had one too many surprises that day, though at least this was a good one.

He had paused just inside the circle of the porch light and rubbed a somewhat sheepish hand on the back of his neck. "Well, I sort of... moved back. I'm in the process of it, at least."

"Why on earth would you do that?" she asked. She winced when she realized how the words might have sounded. "Don't get me wrong, I'm glad you're back, but I thought you were happy out by the ocean, working underwater. That's what you'd always dreamed of."

Nick had left almost as soon as they graduated high school to go to South Carolina and learn how to be an underwater welder. They had dated all through their senior year and he had asked her to come with him, but she had turned him down. At the time, she hadn't wanted to leave her parents and the life she knew. She did regret it occasionally, but less and less as the years went by. She was happy here in Flatstone. It was her home. She couldn't imagine having the same sense of peace and belonging anywhere else.

"I don't know if you heard, but my dad's not doing great. He's not able to live on his own anymore, so he had to move in with my sister. She lives in Ann Arbor, closer to the doctors he needs."

"I hadn't heard," she said. "I'm sorry about that."

"Really, he shouldn't have lived alone as long as he did. He still wouldn't have left, if I hadn't agreed to take over the machine shop and take care of the house for him."

"How long will you be here?"

He shrugged. "Indefinitely. I told him I'd stay here and take care of everything, and I'm not about to go back on my word while he's still breathing. Samantha is taking care of him; I figured the least I can do is take care of the property and business up here. It will be a change, but it's not all bad. I hadn't realized how good it would be to come back. South Carolina never felt like home to me, not like Michigan does."

"Well, I'm glad you're here, even if it isn't in the best of circumstances. Did you really drive all the way out here just to say hi to me? Why don't you come up here on the porch? We can sit and talk on the swing, instead of standing around like two strangers."

He grinned and came up the porch steps, joining her on the long wooden swing that was older than she was. The wood creaked beneath their weight, but it held fast. "Honestly, I spent all day working on the house. Dad had really started to let it go. I needed a break and when Mary said you were still living at the farm, I decided to swing by. I figured at the very least I could give you my cell phone number. I know you've probably got your own life and family, but I'd still like to catch up over a cup of coffee, sometime. For old time's sake."

"Well, you're right that I've got my own life. I own a business and raise alpacas, both of which keep me pretty busy. But it's just me living out here, for now at least. I've been seeing someone for the past couple years, though, and I think it might last."

"That's great," he said, giving her a warm smile. "I'm happy for you, Jo. It sounds like you've done well for yourself."

"How about you?" she asked. "Any little Nicks running around?"

"No. I never managed to make any relationship stick. I was too focused on work, I guess." He shrugged. "I'm a little embarrassed to admit it, but I think I'm actually going to miss my job more than I'll miss any of the friends I made down there. That's my fault, not theirs; I never really took the time to build good relationships with anyone."

"Well, I hope you take more time for that now that you're back," she said. "You're going to be pretty lonely if you don't make any close friends in a town this small." She frowned, thinking of Rose and Andrea. She would have to go over tomorrow and see if Rose was doing all right. Maybe she could try her hand at baking something for the older woman. She wasn't very good at it – she greatly preferred other types of cooking – but it was the effort that counted, wasn't it?

"Hey, are you all right?" Nick asked. "Is this a bad time for you? I can leave."

"No, it's not you," she said with a sigh. "I… I found a dead woman earlier today." She went on to tell him about Andrea and was surprised to find that she was tearing up as she spoke. By the end of her story she was crying, the tears that hadn't come earlier streaming down her face.

"Hey, it's all right," he said, reaching out and pulling her into a tentative hug. She sniffled, trying to get herself under control. She didn't cry frequently, and hated doing it around other people, but seeing Andrea had unearthed all sorts of bad memories for her.

In the end, it was the flash of light across her face and the sound of another vehicle pulling up to the house that made her pull away. She looked over to see a car pull up next to Nick's truck, unable to see anything but the headlights in the dark. She rose from her seat, wondering who it could be. Two unexpected visitors in one night was almost unheard of for her. A car door slammed, and a dark figure stepped in front of the headlights, his front nothing but a shadow.

"Really, Jo?" The annoyed voice rang out through the night. She recognized it immediately. Cole. Her stomach dropped immediately. She had completely forgotten about their date earlier that evening.

CHAPTER FIVE

"I'm so sorry, Cole," she said, moving forward. "I completely forgot, but I can explain –"

"I don't think I need any explanations, Josephina," he snapped. Before she could say anything else, he turned on his heel and walked the short distance around to the driver's side door, which he opened and then shut with a slam after getting in. A moment later, the tires spun, kicking gravel out at the porch as he backed up forcefully and turned the car around before taking off back down the driveway.

Consumed with guilt – *how* could she have forgotten their date? – she turned back to Nick, who was standing awkwardly on the porch. "I'd better get going," he said. "Wait just a second, though, and I'll get something out of my truck to write my number on."

She watched as he walked over to the truck, where he rooted around for a moment before returning with a piece of paper that had a phone number scrawled on it. He handed it over, shifted on his feet, and said, "I guess I'll see you around?"

"Yeah," she said numbly as she took the paper. She forced a smile to her lips. "It was good to see you again, Nick. I'll give you a call in a couple of days once things have settled down here."

She watched as he drove away, feeling suddenly very alone as she trudged over to the fence. She opened the gate and walked through it to the barn, pulling the barn door open and grabbing a bucket of grain to lure the alpacas in. They would get to spend the night warm and cozy with all of their alpaca friends in the barn, the new cria snuggled between them, while she was alone in her silent house, her boyfriend quite possibly thinking about breaking up with her, and her neighbor mourning her deceased friend a house away.

Jo's mood didn't improve the next morning. She had sent text after text to Cole and had even tried calling him once the sun was up, but he was ignoring her thoroughly. She wished he would just give her a chance to explain. Yes, it was bad that she had forgotten their date, but she had found a dead body in Rose's house. She thought that deserved a little bit of sympathy, at least.

Moping around wouldn't do anything for her, though. She had a lot to do today before she could even begin to think about tracking down her boyfriend and explaining why she had been so distracted last night. As usual, the animals needed to be taken care of before anything else. She couldn't put that off no matter how bad she was feeling.

Once the female alpacas were let out, the new cria taking an unsteady trot around the pasture, and both sets of alpacas were fed and their water was changed, she went back inside and began getting ready for her own day by gathering one of her more recent crochet projects, an afghan, from her living room and storing it in her crochet bag. It was Wednesday, which meant she had her crochet club after work today.

She was ready to head into town with enough time to spare that she was able to walk over to Rose's house first. Once she was on the porch, she knocked on the door. Inside, she heard a voice call out, "Come in!"

Turning the handle, she stepped inside. Rose was sitting in her favorite chair in the living room, looking through a magazine. She looked up and gave Jo a serious look when she came in.

"How are you doing, dear? I feel so bad that you had to see that yesterday. It can't have been easy."

Jo suppressed a shudder. "It's not something I want to repeat. I feel so bad for Andrea, and all of her friends and family. How are you holding up? I barely knew her. It was still horrible to find her like that, but it can't be anything compared to what you're experiencing."

"It's been hard, but she's not the first friend I lost," Rose said softly. "I don't want to say you get used to it, because you don't, but I've come to accept that when it's someone's time, there's nothing you can do about it."

"Do the police think it was natural causes, then?" Jo asked. She figured they must – she didn't think they would let Rose stay in her house if they were investigating it as a homicide. Her friend nodded.

"I think so. They don't know the cause of death yet, but there wasn't any sign of a struggle, and she wasn't injured at all. She just... collapsed. A paramedic told me she probably didn't suffer."

"I think they were right," Jo said, trying to be gentle. "Whatever happened, it must've been sudden. If she had a stroke or an aneurysm, there wouldn't have been anything anyone could do."

Rose sighed. "I hope you're right. I suppose we might never know for sure. Thanks for stopping by, Jo. You're a great friend, I hope you know that."

Jo gave her a tight smile, not feeling like she deserved the praise. She had left her boyfriend waiting for her in Port Austin yesterday evening, after all.

Mornings at Full Skein Ahead were usually slow and sleepy, and today was no exception. She was able to get some work done on her afghan, while she sat behind the counter, taking the occasional break to chat with her customers, either inquiring after the projects of her regulars or going over what the different types of yarn were used for with her new customers.

If there was one thing she loved, it was talking about her craft, and she discovered that most other people felt the same way. Whether their passion was knitting and crocheting, or if they had a love for handcrafted items, she never seemed to run out of things to say to most of her customers.

It was only a few minutes before one, and the end of her shift, when her cell phone started buzzing in her purse. She normally didn't answer it during working hours, so she ignored the first two calls. But when whoever it was called back a third time, she finally realized it might be important. Suddenly worried, she scrabbled through her purse to find the phone. The number was local, but unfamiliar, and she answered it with a cautious, "Hello?"

"Hi, Jo. It's Rose." Her voice was weak. "I'm at the hospital. I'm okay, at least I'm going to be. I just wanted to let you know so if you heard about it from someone else you wouldn't worry."

"You're at the hospital? What happened?"

"I started feeling ill a little bit after you left." Rose's voice was shaky when she spoke again. "It... it was the lemonade, Jo. I'm almost certain that's what killed Andrea. I had a glass this morning and an hour later I started feeling strange. I felt weak, almost like I couldn't breathe, and my vision got fuzzy. I called an ambulance when the feeling didn't go away after a few minutes. It wasn't until I was at the hospital, and they started asking me questions about what I'd had to eat and drink that morning that I made the connection. Andrea had two glasses of lemonade when I was sitting with her yesterday. And from the looks of it, she might have had even more, since the lemonade was still sitting out on the counter when she collapsed, and you said there was glass spilled next to her."

"If it was the lemonade, wouldn't you have gotten sick yesterday, too?"

"I didn't have any yesterday. My stomach was bothering me, and too much citrus always makes it worse. It's the only thing I can think of. I told the police, and they will be taking the rest of the lemonade in for testing. Could you do me a favor, though? I'm not very good at looking things up on the internet. Can you see if a batch of bad lemons could have the effects I described? The lemonade only had lemon, sugar, and water in it, and I can't imagine the sugar, or the water was bad."

"Of course," Jo said. "I'll do some research for you. Give me a call if you need anything in the meantime, okay? And, let me know if you want a visitor."

"Thank you, dear. I've got Harper helping me for now, but if I need anything else, I'll let you know."

They said their goodbyes and Jo ended the call, but she turned the volume up on her phone so if Rose called back, she would be able to answer it right away. She was worried about her neighbor but didn't know what to think about what she had said about the lemonade. Who had ever heard of lemonade killing someone?

She pulled up the browser on her cell phone and began typing in various queries about lemons. The only link she found to any health issues caused by lemonade was food poisoning from expired lemon juice, but the symptoms of that were the same as any other food poisoning.

Still, she couldn't dismiss Rose's concerns completely. It did seem like a bit too much of a coincidence for Andrea to have passed away shortly after having a couple glasses of the lemonade, and the next day Rose got sick after having the same. She was glad, all of a sudden, that she had asked for only water when she ate pie at Rose's house. It was frightening to think that she might have met the same fate as Andrea, if she had accepted the offer for lemonade.

At least, the police were going to analyze it. She didn't know how long it would take, but it meant they would get answers, eventually.

The bell rang and Kaylee came in, a cheerful smile on her face. Jo forced her attention away from the phone to smile and wave at the younger woman, who bustled over to the counter with her laptop. Kaylee was a college student, and Jo was fine with her doing her homework while at work, as long as she focused on customers when they came in.

"Busy morning?" she asked as she stashed her purse behind the counter.

"It was about average," Jo said. "Don't forget, I'm hosting the crochet club here today. People should start arriving in about ten minutes."

"All right. Do you have any more samples you want me to put out? It looks like we are running low."

"Not yet, but I should have some more by next week," Jo said. "If we run out, just tell people to come back in on Tuesday, and we should have some."

Whenever she made a new batch of yarn, she usually kept a small portion of it as a sample. That way, if someone was interested in a type of yarn they had never used before, they could take the free sample home with them before committing to buying enough for their project. Some of the yarn she sold was expensive, and she didn't accept returns either, so the samples were a good compromise.

While Kaylee situated herself for the day, Jo moved toward the back of the store. There was a round table and a few chairs set up so people could sit and knit or crochet if they wanted to. The back room stored more folding chairs, and Jo took these out, placing them around the table, and then got out the laminated sign that said *Flatstone Crochet Club! Ask us about joining.*

The club was small right now, with only five people other than her in it, but sometimes they had nearly twice that many people. It just depended on who happened to be free at any given time. They always did their best to make sure their meetings were scheduled so the maximum number of interested parties could join.

Laurie was the first to arrive, bustling inside and putting her yarn bag down on the table as she greeted Jo and cheerfully began chatting about how the kitchen renovation she and her husband were doing was going and then asked about the baby alpacas. Jo told her one of them had given birth. Out the front window, Jo saw Emma, their youngest member, chaining her bike to the bike stand before coming in as well. She gave both Laurie and Jo a shy greeting before taking her project out of her bag.

The others arrived over the next few minutes: Marge, Darlene, Lorraine, and Wendy. Their ages ranged from sixteen to over eighty, with Lorraine being the oldest member. They came from all walks of life, some married and some not, some with children and some determinedly child-free. The one thing they all had in common was a love for crocheting.

They spent a few minutes chatting with each other, until the clock hit one-thirty. Then, all eyes turned to Jo, who pulled a couple of papers out of her own yarn bag and put them on the table.

"Before we begin, we have a couple of things to discuss. Next week is our last scheduled meeting, so I'm going to need everyone to email me with the best days and times for you. Please give me at least two to three different options, if possible. As usual, I'll try to find days that work for everyone. For those of you who sell your handmade items here, we are updating our sales contract – nothing major, but we are going to need your signatures, again. I'll leave the contracts on the table in case you want to take them home and look them over before signing. The changes go into effect at the beginning of August, so there's no big hurry. Other than that, I think we're good to go. Any questions?"

Wendy, a quiet woman who was the mother of three rowdy boys, raised her hand. "You're neighbors with Rose Cantrell, right? Is it true that she killed someone yesterday?"

Jo blinked. "Sorry, what?"

Wendy flushed. "It's just that my son, Adam, mentioned that he was riding past your house yesterday. He told me he saw a lot of police vehicles there and that one of his friends told him it was because the old lady who lived in the house had killed someone."

"I'm afraid your son's friend was mistaken," Jo said, trying to keep the surprise out of her voice. The thought of Rose committing murder was just absurd. "A woman did die, but it was an accidental death."

"Who was it?" Laurie chimed in.

"I don't know if I should say," Jo said. "I'm sure her family doesn't want to deal with rumors spreading."

"None of us will let the word get out," Lorraine said softly. "I'm with Laurie. I want to know if it was someone I was friends with."

Jo bit back a sigh. "It was Andrea Bowman."

Immediately, chatter started making its way around the table. Jo winced at some of the speculation she heard. The only person who wasn't participating in the talk was Emma, who was studiously working on her sweater.

"Excuse me," Jo said, clearing her throat. "If you want to talk about this on your own time, go ahead, but it's not something I want to spend the afternoon discussing. I was the one who found her body, and I don't want to keep reliving it if it's all the same to you."

They quieted down, looking a bit ashamed. "Sorry," Laurie said. "You're right, we shouldn't be focusing on such dark matters. We are here to relax and share what progress we've made over the last week. I'm almost halfway done with my cardigan now…"

Relieved, Jo picked up her afghan and began working on it, letting the soothing conversation wash over her. She wasn't necessarily surprised that rumors were already spreading about what happened to Andrea, but she was disappointed. Rose as a murderer? She scoffed. The idea was absolutely ridiculous.

CHAPTER SIX

After crochet club ended, Jo packed up her things and got in her car, checking her phone to make sure she hadn't missed any calls from Rose. Rose hadn't called her, and neither had Cole.

She tried calling him again, but it went straight to voicemail. She grumbled, checked the time, and sighed. He did a lot of work from home, but he also had showings at any and all hours throughout the day, so there was no telling if he would be at his house right now. She decided she might as well give it a try. Worst case, she was out a few minutes of her time. Best case, she could take the opportunity to explain exactly what had happened the night before. With any luck, he would forgive her. She felt terrible for forgetting their date, but it wasn't as if she had meant to. If he couldn't forgive her for being traumatized after finding a woman *dead*, well, maybe she would be the one ignoring him.

Filled with righteous indignation, she made the short drive to his house. He lived on the lower floor of a small duplex in town. She took a deep breath as she walked up to the door, trying to convince herself that things weren't really all that bad between them. He was just mad because he didn't know what had happened. Once she explained herself, she was sure things would go back to normal between them.

She knocked on the door and was raising her fist to knock again when it finally opened. Relieved, she felt a smile break out over her face, only to be halted in its tracks when he spoke, running a hand through his hair.

"Jo, what are you doing? If I wanted to talk to you, I would've answered your calls."

"I needed to talk to you."

He sighed. "I figured, from all of the messages and calls you've been sending me. But I don't want to talk to you. Last night was the last straw. I don't care what explanation you have –"

"Please, Cole, just give me the chance to tell you what happened," Jo said, suddenly realizing with a drop in her stomach just how serious he was about this. "I swear, it's not what you think."

"Fine," he said, his voice tight. "I'm listening. But don't expect it to change anything."

Both irritated and worried, Jo took a deep breath to try to calm herself down before she told him about finding Andrea. Her voice broke as she spoke, and she included some of what had happened at the crochet club earlier as well. "You have no idea how terrible I feel," she added when she was done. "I never would have left you waiting like that on purpose, and I'm sure after last week you were already mad at me. I don't blame you for feeling like this was the last straw, but I never would have forgotten about our date if I hadn't found Andrea. Seeing her like that…" She shuddered. "It was horrible, and I haven't felt normal since."

His expression softened, but only fractionally. "I'm really sorry that happened to you, Jo, but you're wrong about what the issue was. I was mad about the date, yes, but I figured you had an explanation. I thought something might be wrong with one of the animals or one of your friends, and I was coming over to make sure everything was okay and see if you needed any help. No, the problem was that man you were with, Jo. How do you think I felt when you skipped out on our date and then I drove up your driveway to find you embracing another man? I'm sure that most of what you were saying is true, but that doesn't change the facts. I just can't do this, anymore."

"What are you talking about?" she asked, utterly shocked. "Nick is just a friend. I hadn't seen him for over fifteen years. I didn't even know he was coming over last night; he surprised me. I was only hugging him because I had broken down after telling him about Andrea. It was the first time I cried since it happened, and if I had been standing next to an alpaca when it happened, I would have hugged it, instead. Nothing happened, I swear. I can't even believe you would think that of me."

"I don't know what to believe," he said with a sigh. "It doesn't matter. I realized last night that I just don't want to do this, anymore. I'm never going to be the most important thing in your life, and I can't keep waiting for that to change, because I've realized it won't."

"Yes, you are," she said, on the verge of tears. "You're so important to me, Cole."

"No, I'm not." He gave her an even look. "You have the alpacas, your farm, your knitting and crocheting, your business, your friends... They all seem to come before me. I can understand that. That's the sort of life you've chosen. But it's not the sort of life I want. I want someone who's going to be focused on our relationship, and I've come to terms with the fact that you are not that. I don't have any ill wishes toward you. I think you're a wonderful woman in a lot of ways, Jo, but I'm done."

With that, he turned toward the door. Jo opened her mouth to call him back, but no words would come out. What could she say? Could she beg him not to do this? Did she really want to be with someone who didn't want to be with her?

Deciding she didn't, she shut her mouth again, and Cole went back into his house without another word.

CHAPTER SEVEN

Jo drove back home slowly, pausing every now and then to wipe away a tear. She was feeling a horrible mixture of sadness and anger. Mostly, though, what she felt was self-pity. Why wasn't she good enough? When had their relationship gone so wrong? She had thought things were fine. Sure, they had been going through a rough patch lately, but overall, hadn't things been good?

She was still sniffing when she pulled up her driveway, but the tears had mostly stopped. She had a lot to do, between checking on the cria and catching up on some spinning. Life didn't grind to a halt just because she was sad.

She met her eyes in the rearview mirror before she got out of her car and wondered if maybe Cole had a point. Yes, she was sad that their relationship was over, but life had to go on. She would cry over him, but it wasn't the end of the world. Maybe he wanted someone who would be unable to function properly if they had a breakup. She just wasn't that kind of person. She had been raised to believe that things that needed to be done, got done regardless of what was going on in the rest of her life. Being upset didn't mean you couldn't lift bags of feed or move the animals into a new pasture. It just meant you might want to carry a handkerchief while you're doing it in case you started crying.

Taking a deep, bracing breath, she got out of the car. The female alpacas were all contentedly eating or lying down, relaxing. Over on the other side of the yard, Darwin watched her with his ears pricked up, while behind him Yeti and Coal were nibbling at the hay she had thrown in there that morning.

"Hey, you," she said, going over to pat Darwin's neck. "I'm going to head out to check the fences in the other pastures, then how do you feel about getting some new grass to graze on? You're running a bit low in here."

Alpacas weren't very hard on natural foliage. They had padded feet, unlike goats and sheep, and they didn't eat very much for animals of their size, but nonetheless, it was good to rotate their pastures occasionally, so the grass had time to regrow.

"Hey, Jo!"

She looked up to see Harper waving at her from Rose's porch. She waved back and called out, "Hi, Harper!"

"Do you have a minute?"

Jo hesitated, then shrugged. "Sure. I'll be right over."

She figured Harper wanted to talk about Rose. It felt almost unbelievable that it was only earlier that morning that Rose had called to tell her she was in the hospital. So much had happened since then. Her chores could wait for a few more minutes.

She walked around the pasture and started the short hike across the lawn toward her neighbor's house. Darwin and then Yeti came up to follow her along the fence line, and she could see Harper grinning at what must be a funny looking procession. Alpacas were cute, but they weren't graceful looking creatures. In fact, they looked like something out of a children's book, especially when they were shaved with the tops of their heads left fluffy, like hers were.

"How is Rose doing?" she asked when she was in easy talking range to Harper.

"The doctors said she's going to be okay. They were able to treat her pretty quickly once she mentioned her concerns about the lemonade." Harper frowned. "It's really strange, I don't know what could have happened. The treatment they gave her is supposed to negate consumed toxins and poisons, and it worked. They're going to keep her for observation for the next day or two, but they don't expect any complications."

"She called me while I was at work and I tried looking up similar incidents involving lemons or lemonade, and I couldn't find anything," Jo said, leaning against the porch railing. "Hopefully, the police will turn something up."

"Yeah, but what are they going to find?" Harper asked, a worried look on her face.

"What do you mean?" Jo asked.

The younger woman hesitated. "It's just… Aunt Rose is getting older, you know? What if… what if she made a mistake? What if she thought she was grabbing sugar or some extra lemon juice, but instead put something poisonous in the lemonade? When I worked at the nursing home, I once had a resident who put salt in their coffee for a week and couldn't understand why it tasted so bad."

"You think that she put some sort of poison in the lemonade?"

"Not on purpose," Harper said hurriedly. "But it's possible she made a mistake, isn't it? Sometimes when you get old, your mind does strange things. If she did, and it turns out that she is responsible for what happened to Andrea, what will the police do to her?"

"I don't think Rose would've made a mistake like that," Jo said uncomfortably. This conversation was too close to the same one she'd had with Wendy earlier. "She still bakes a lot, and none of her pies or muffins have turned out bad, have they? I'm pretty sure if she can still put together a pie on her own, she's not going to make a mistake with something as simple as lemonade."

"I hope you're right," Harper said. "But if she didn't do it, who did? There has to have been something in that lemonade other than lemons, water, and sugar for it to affect both her and Andrea like that."

"Are you saying you think someone poisoned the lemonade on purpose?"

"I don't know what I'm saying," Harper said with a sigh. "I'm just worried about what the police are going to find, that's all. I know it seems far-fetched that someone might have poisoned the lemonade, but if you think about all of the problems Andrea's been having with her divorce, it's not too unbelievable that someone would want to hurt her."

"I don't know much about the divorce," Jo admitted. "What exactly happened with that?"

"Well, she found out her husband was having an affair, and from what I overheard her telling Rose, she made out very well in the divorce hearing. When I first heard that she had died, I wondered if her husband – her ex-husband, sorry – had something to do with it. I don't see how he could have, since he would've had to do something to the lemonade, and that was sitting safely in Rose's fridge all morning, but I can't help but wonder if there's a connection there. He's the one who would benefit most from her death, after all. He wouldn't have to pay alimony or lose the house."

"I still think it was probably an accidental death," Jo said. "If she had been found dead in her own house, I guess I might agree with what you're saying, but I think it's a bit far-fetched that her ex-husband would sneak into Rose's house just to poison some lemonade that his ex-wife may or may not drink. It seems much more likely that all of the stress of the divorce caught up to her, and that Rose's problem is unrelated."

"You're probably right," Harper said. "I've probably just read too many thrillers. Still, I'll let you know when the police tell us what they found. They said it could be a couple of weeks – they had to send the lemonade out to another city for testing."

"Well, whatever they end up finding, I hope it puts all of our questions to rest," Jo said. "I'd better get going – I've got a lot to do this evening. I'll see you around, Harper. Tell Rose that I've got my phone's volume turned up just in case she needs anything."

"I will," Harper promised. "See you later, Jo."

CHAPTER EIGHT

She spent the next couple of days stuck in the quiet routine of her life. Without dinner dates and lunches with Cole to break up the monotony, things settled into a rhythm that was comfortable, if boring. She walked the fence line to make sure the fences were all in good condition, then moved the alpacas, taking the males to the pasture immediately behind the house and putting the females in the one on the other side of the barn, so they could still be let in at night. One of the fences in the far back pasture had broken when a tree fell on it sometime earlier that year, so she added that to her list of things to get done. She spent some time simply watching the alpacas as they frolicked through the new grass and felt their happiness ease her heart. Her chickens, which milled around during the day but returned to the small coop she had made for them in the barn on their own in the evening, squabbled and clucked, living their own lives, mostly unconcerned with her. She gathered their eggs in the morning, spun yarn out of fleece and wool, and chatted with her customers at the yarn shop like usual.

Her life wasn't any different than it had been before, but somehow it seemed emptier. She realized that she was lonely. She had grown used to having Cole around and missed the sense of companionship. Sure, she had friends, but they all had their own lives, too. They met once or twice a week for crochet club and had the occasional brunch or lunch together, but in terms of constant companionship, she was lacking.

That was why, when she found Nick's cell phone number scribbled on the piece of paper she had shoved in her pocket when she was putting clothes in the washer, she decided to give him a call. It was midday, and she had just gotten back from the morning shift at the yarn shop. She only realized belatedly that he might be busy at work, but he answered quickly enough when she rang.

"Hi, Nick," she said when he picked up. "It's me – Jo."

"Hey, Jo." She heard a clatter and he muttered something, but when he spoke again, his voice was clear. "Sorry about that – I was up on a ladder when you called."

"Is now not a good time?"

"No, no, it's great. I'm just repainting the living room at my dad's place. It's about time I took a break, anyway. I'm glad you called. I was worried you wouldn't, after the other night."

"I just had a lot going on," she said. "If you still want to get together and catch up, let me know when you're free. You have my number now, so feel free to call me, anytime."

"Are you free now?" he asked. "I've been working on this house all day, and I am starting to go stir crazy."

"I've just got a few chores to do around the house, and a fence to start repairs on, but I'll be free in a couple hours."

"I can come help you with that fence, if you'd like," Nick said. "I'd rather spend the afternoon working outside, instead of stuck in a room filled with paint fumes."

"Are you sure?"

"Yeah. I figure I owe you some help anyway, to make up for my badly-timed visit. I didn't mean to cause any issues."

"It wasn't your fault," she said. "I'm glad you stopped by. It's great that you're back in town."

"It's nice being back, too," he said. "So, should I head over?"

"Yeah, it will be nice to have some help. I'll see you in a bit."

She got most of her chores done by the time Nick arrived, so that she would be able to focus on repairing the fence. She was just loading some spare planks of wood into a wheelbarrow when he pulled up the driveway in his truck. He got out and paused to look around before walking over to her.

"Where did all the alpacas go?" he asked, careful not to trip over a chicken that ran across his path.

"I rotated them to different pastures. It will give the grass a few weeks to recover, and then I'll move them back. Oh, you have to see the new baby. You haven't seen her yet. Come on, follow me."

Leaving the wheelbarrow, she led him back around the barn to where the female alpacas were lounging in the fresh grass. The cria, who was much steadier on her legs now, was skipping around the field, running back to her mother every so often when something startled her. Jo opened the gate and let the two of them through before approaching the young alpaca. She made soothing noises as she neared. It took a couple of seconds, but eventually the curious cria approached, cautiously.

"She is pretty cute," he said with a grin, crouching down to pat her soft, fluffy fur. "Does she have a name?"

"Not yet," Jo said. One of the older alpacas, Marcy, came ambling over to see if she had any treats in her pocket, and she patted her absentmindedly. "I think I'll wait to see a bit more of her personality come out. Since she's female, she'll be staying here. The males I usually sell to other farms – three is more than enough for me."

"Do you have any hired help, or do you take care of them all yourself?" Nick asked, rising to his feet.

"I do it all myself," she said as they walked back toward the gate. "It keeps me busy, but the yarn shop is only open from ten to five, and only from twelve to three on Sundays. We're almost never busy enough to need more than one person at the shop, which means I've got plenty of time to care for the farm, too. There's almost always something I have to do, but I manage to keep up with it well enough."

They returned for the wheelbarrow, and Nick helped her load up the rest of the supplies for the fence, then they made their way to the back pasture where the broken fence was.

"This is a nice parcel of land," Nick said as they worked. "You've got plenty of space, and a good mix of trees and open areas."

"I'm lucky I was able to inherit it," Jo said. "Land around here has started selling for a pretty penny. I probably wouldn't have been able to afford it, otherwise."

"Land prices everywhere are going up," he said with a sigh. "As nice as it is to have property, I do wish my father would agree to sell some of his. He hasn't used most of it for years, and now that he's not even living here, it seems pointless to keep it. Even if he agreed to sell just half of it, we'd be able to put the money toward a good care facility for him."

"That's probably why he doesn't want you to sell it," she said. "I'm sure he'd rather be living with Samantha than in a facility with strangers."

Nick grinned at her. "You're probably right about that, come to think of it."

The rumbling sound of an old diesel engine sounded across the field on the other side of the fence. It was fallow this year, but next year would be ripe with crops. She always liked watching the farming equipment work, even though the dust it kicked up into the air made her cough.

The truck was rattling across the field toward them. It slowed down and the driver waved, and she recognized Dale Fisher. He owned most of the land out there – he grew corn, soybeans, and grain on a few hundred acres across the surrounding area. Her parcel of land was just a tiny divot cut out of it, though Rose owned much more land.

The truck slowed further until Dale turned it off, popping out and walking over to greet her.

"Oh, I'm glad you spotted the fence. I was going to tell you about it, but it must've slipped my mind. I hope you haven't had any escapees because of it," he said, his hands in his pockets and a brimmed hat protecting his eyes from the sun.

"No, I noticed it when I did my walk around before moving the alpacas to their new pastures," she said. "How are things going for you? It's been a dry summer so far."

He sighed, pressing his lips together and making a popping sound with them. "Water costs are killing me. Most of my land is higher up, and since it hasn't rained much, the ground is dry. If only all my crops were in nice, low land like you have out here. If only Rose would sell…" He trailed off, shaking his head. "I'll just have to hope the drought breaks."

"Well, I'll keep my fingers crossed for rain," she promised.

"Thanks, Jo." He rubbed at his eyes with a sigh. "Sorry, dry eyes. Some wetter weather might help that, too. Anyway, I just thought I'd swing by and say hi when I saw you. I'd better get going, though." He nodded, then headed back to his truck. Pausing, he turned back to her. "Oh, my wife wanted me to tell you she's going to be looking for some sort of special yarn for a baby blanket pretty soon. Her cousin's expecting, and she wants to give them something homemade."

"I'll give her a call and see what I can do for her," Jo promised. "See you around, Dale."

He raised a hand in a wave goodbye and hopped into his truck, starting the engine, and pulling away.

"I forgot what that was like," Nick said beside her, chuckling. He picked up a plank and held it in place while she started nailing it into the post. "You can't go anywhere in town without seeing somebody you know."

"I like it," she said decisively as she hammered the last nail in. "There's not much privacy, but there's plenty of trust, and that's worth a lot."

CHAPTER NINE

Spending the afternoon with Nick was pleasant. Part of her felt a little bit bad for spending so much time with another man, but she had to keep reminding herself that she and Cole were over and done with. He had made it clear that he didn't want to be involved in the relationship anymore, and she wasn't about to beg him to come back. In time, maybe, they could be friends, but for now, she thought it best that they give each other some space. Besides, Nick was just an acquaintance, an old friend that she was getting to know again. Sure, they had dated back when they were seniors in high school, but that was a long time ago and they were different people now. Besides, they had been best friends long before that. Spending time with him was easy. He was used to physical labor and helped her fix the fence and do a few other chores around the farm without complaint. He was curious about the animals and respected her know-how when she showed him how to do something. In turn, she trusted his word when he looked over the old baler she used for harvesting the small alfalfa field at the front of her property and said it needed some new welds. She promised to bring it down to the machine shop when she got the chance.

The day after he helped her with the fence, Rose returned home. Jo was overjoyed that her neighbor was out of the hospital and went over with a nice, baby blue skein of freshly dyed yarn as a welcome back gift. When she asked Rose how she was feeling, the older woman assured her that she was fine, then said, "Now, the real important question is, are you bringing that friend of yours to the funeral?"

"Laurie?" Jo asked, blinking.

Rose chuckled. "No. A little bird told me that you've been spending some time with Nicholas Moore, again. I remember when you were just a little thing and he was over all the time, getting in trouble with you over on your parents' farm. I always thought the two of you were meant to be."

"It's not like that, Rose," Jo sputtered. "Just because Cole and I aren't together anymore doesn't mean I'm going to jump right into another relationship. Nick was just helping me with a fence repair. I haven't seen him for years, and I'll admit it's nice to spend some time with an old friend, because that's all we are. Friends."

"If you say so," Rose said, looking like she didn't believe Jo in the slightest. "Anyway, you should bring him to the funeral. You know how people will talk if he doesn't go, and I doubt he'll go on his own. Andrea used to babysit him when he was younger."

"She did?" Jo asked. She shook her head. She shouldn't be surprised; it was a small town. Rose had babysat Jo plenty of times when she was a child. "Well, I guess I can see if he wants to go with me. You don't want me to go with you and Harper?"

"I'm going to go early. I'd like to have a little bit of time to say goodbye to her before the service starts."

Her throat feeling thicker all the sudden, Jo nodded. "I understand." The funeral was tomorrow, and it would have been almost a week since Andrea had passed away. Jo hoped against hope that no one would say anything to Rose about some of the rumors that had been spreading about her. She still couldn't believe Wendy's son had heard that Rose had killed Andrea. Rose would be hurt if she heard it, even if it was just something a troublemaker made up.

When she got home, she sent a text message to Nick, asking if he wanted to go to the funeral with her. He agreed, so she set her alarm early the next morning, ensuring that she would have the time to take care of the animals and get ready for the funeral before she had to leave to meet him.

There was only one funeral home in Flatstone, and this wasn't the first time Jo had been there. It was, however, the busiest she had ever seen it. Most of the deaths in Flatstone occurred either due to old age or accidents – car crashes, farming incidents, or the occasional boating accident. The fact that Andrea had died under mysterious circumstances and the rumors that were spreading around town like wildfire ensured that more people than usual would come to her funeral.

Jo and Nick went inside for the viewing. Jo spotted Rose chatting with one of Andrea's family members. She thought the woman might be Andrea's older sister, but she wasn't familiar enough with her to be sure. Not wanting to interrupt, she simply moved up to Andrea's coffin, silently paying respects to the other woman, before going with Nick to take a seat toward the back. They had arrived only a few minutes before the service was supposed to start, neither of them having known Andrea well, and it wasn't long before people began settling down. While the pastor talked about Andrea's life, Jo looked around the room, recognizing most of the faces. One in particular caught her eye – Cole. She wondered what he was doing there and remembered with a jolt that he had sold the Bowmans their house only last year.

She shifted in her seat, hoping that he hadn't seen her yet, but the movement seemed to catch his attention. He looked around and frowned when he met her eye. She winced when she realized that sitting right next to Nick probably wouldn't do much to convince him that she had been telling the truth when she said Nick was just an old friend. Biting back a sigh, she forced her attention away from him and looked forward.

Her gaze was caught by the sight of Bradley Bowman, Andrea's ex-husband. He was sitting near the front but had turned his head to say something to the person sitting next to him, one of his grown children. She was surprised to see him there, having heard just how badly their relationship had ended, but supposed that it made sense that he would want to be there with his children to comfort them after their loss. When his son turned back to face the front, she thought she caught a flash of annoyance on Bradley's face before he returned his attention to the service. She felt a surge of sadness for Andrea. Bradley obviously didn't want to be there, which meant he probably hadn't wanted to be around much when she was alive, either.

Once the service was over, people began slowly leaving the room, the family and closest friends staying behind for a final goodbye. Jo and Nick waited just outside the building for Rose – Jo wanted to see how she was doing before she headed home. Harper joined them not long after, looking glad to be out of the stuffy building.

"Oh, Jo, I didn't see you earlier."

"We were in the back," Jo told her. "I saw you two, but Rose was having a conversation with someone, and I didn't want to interrupt."

"Well, Rose and I were talking about going out for lunch afterward. Do you want to come with us?"

"I'd be happy to, but Nick and I drove together." She turned to look at him. "What do you think? Do you want to go to lunch with Rose and Harper?"

He shrugged. "Sure. I've got some things to do this evening, but I'm free until then."

Harper looked at him for the first time, seeming to realize that he wasn't just a bystander. "Hi, I'm Harper. I work for Rose and am also her niece."

Nick shook her hand. "Nicholas Moore. You look familiar. Have we met?"

"I don't think so," Harper said. "I didn't grow up here, and I don't know where else you would have seen me. Anyway, if you'll excuse me, I'd better go find Rose. I'll tell her the two of you are coming along to lunch. See you in a few minutes, Jo."

She left just as suddenly as she had come. Jo watched her go with a raised eyebrow, then turned back to Nick, deciding that Harper's somewhat strange behavior could probably be excused by her concern for Rose, who would be grieving her friend.

"I guess this is your official welcome back to Flatstone," she said to Nick. "Now that everyone has seen you at the funeral, word's going to spread quickly."

He grimaced. "Hopefully, the novelty wears off soon. I've been enjoying the peace and quiet of no one knowing I'm here."

CHAPTER TEN

Lunch was at a little diner called Patsy's Place. Jo had been there countless times, and the waitress who served them was a regular at her yarn shop. They chatted for a few minutes, the woman giving Rose her condolences about Andrea, before she took their drink orders. Nick looked down at his menu, a wistful expression on his face.

"I can't believe the last time I ate here was right after my graduation from high school."

"Rose told me you moved away," Harper said. "Where did you go?"

"South Carolina," he said. "I went to trade school and got certified in underwater welding."

"That's interesting," Harper said, turning her attention back to her menu as if it was anything but.

Jo had never known Harper to be anything but polite, so this sudden strangeness bordering on rudeness toward Nick was surprising. She didn't say anything about it, not wanting to bring any bad feelings up so soon after a funeral. Instead, she turned to Rose.

"How are you doing?" she asked.

"I'm holding up," her neighbor said with a weak smile. "It was a beautiful service, don't you think?"

"It really was," Jo said. "Have you heard anything back from the police yet?"

"No, not yet. It's going to be a while, I think. Harper thinks someone might have added something to the lemonade, but I don't see who could have done that. It's not as if I have strangers tramping through my house all day. It has to have been the lemons. They must have gone bad, somehow."

"Sorry, but I'm confused," Nick said. "What is this about lemons? What do the police have to do with it?"

Jo realized that she had told him about finding Andrea but hadn't really updated him on any of what had happened since. She quickly told him about Rose getting ill and her theory that there had been something wrong with the lemonade, since it was the only link between her and Andrea.

"I didn't realize it was a suspicious death," Nick said, frowning. "Things must have changed a lot in this town since I left. You have my condolences. That has to be hard for you."

"We don't know for sure it was suspicious," Jo said. "Really, it might be a complete coincidence. It's just between the common denominator of Andrea's death and Rose's illness with the lemonade, and Andrea's recent divorce, it seems like something else might be going on. The police are testing the lemonade now and will get back to Rose once they learn something."

"Lemonade doesn't just kill people, though," Nick said. "And it doesn't make any sense that if someone was trying to kill Andrea, they would poison a drink at Rose's house. There's no way they could be sure the right person would drink it. They could have killed anyone."

"You're all jumping to conclusions far too quickly,"

Rose interrupted. "I said I thought there was something wrong with the lemonade, not that it was poisoned. It was just a bad batch of lemons, that's all."

Harper looked irritated, but Jo decided to change the subject before it evolved into an argument. Reaching for a new subject, she settled on Cole and brought up seeing him at the funeral and the look he had given her. Immediately, Rose latched onto the subject, sending weighted looks over at Nick as she dove way too deeply into Jo's love life.

CHAPTER ELEVEN

After Andrea's funeral, things seemed to calm back down. Life went on, as it always had, and the mystery of what happened to Andrea remained something that Jo wondered about but didn't worry herself too much over. Only time would give them the answers they wanted, and Jo was a patient person.

Friday afternoon, Jo was working in the yarn shop, carefully arranging a couple of handmade scarves on a new display. James, her other employee, had stayed a little bit longer than usual to help her rearrange the store, and he was setting up a display of handwoven baskets in the front. Every so often, Jo glanced outside, feeling eager for the end of the day so she could get back to the farm and enjoy the nice weather.

She liked being outside and loved the fresh air. The door to the yarn shop was propped open, but it wasn't the same as lying in her hammock, strung between two trees, and reading a book. With luck, she would have a few hours to relax this evening, something that didn't happen every day.

When she was done with the scarves, she retreated to the register, where she sipped from her bottle of pop. She was looking down at the sales report from yesterday and didn't notice someone coming into the store until a shadow passed over the paper. She blinked, looked up, and came face-to-face with Nick.

"Oh, hi," she said. "You startled me."

"Sorry," he said. He looked around, seemingly impressed. "This is a really nice place, Jo."

"I love it," she admitted. "I can't imagine yarn holds much interest for you, though."

"I don't knit," he admitted. "But I still think it's impressive that you've done all of this. Building a business from the ground up can't be easy, and you've done a great job."

"Thank you," she said. "Can I get you anything? We keep some cold waters and bottled drinks in a mini fridge behind the register."

"No, I'm fine," he said. "Actually, I came in here to ask you about that girl, Harper."

"What about her?" Jo asked, raising an eyebrow.

"Well, when I first met her, I thought I recognized her. Even though she said I didn't know her, I could have sworn we met before. So, I gave it some thought when I got back home that evening and realized that I had seen her at a nursing home Sam and I visited back when we were trying to figure out what to do about my dad, before deciding to move him in with Sam. It was out in Port Austin. She worked there at the time, and she gave us the tour. I still wasn't a hundred percent certain, so I called the nursing home and asked for her name. It turns out I was right – it was her. And, she had been fired. You'll never believe what they told me about why."

"Don't keep me in suspense," Jo replied, curious despite herself.

"Apparently, she was accused of stealing medication from some of the residents. I'm guessing she pretended not to recognize me in hopes that word wouldn't get out about why she lost her job."

"I always thought she quit so she could come help Rose," Jo said. She frowned. "I wonder if Rose knows the truth."

"I hope she does," Nick said. "I know that there's been some strange stuff going on with what happened to Andrea, so it seemed like something you should know."

"Thanks, Nick," Jo said. She looked down at the sales form from yesterday, biting her lip. She had a lot to think about now. Why was Harper lying to everyone about the reason she had come to stay with Rose? And did it have anything to do with Andrea's death?

CHAPTER TWELVE

Wondering if Harper had been honest with her great aunt, Jo decided to head over to Rose's house after work. Harper's car was there, but when she knocked on the door, Rose was the one who answered.

"What a lovely surprise," she said. "Come on in, dear."

"Thanks," Jo said, stepping inside. "Is now a good time? I have some things I want to talk to you about, but I can always come back later."

"It's fine," Rose said. "What's on your mind?" She took a seat on her overstuffed armchair. Jo perched on the couch, looking around. She strained her ears but didn't hear anyone else in the house.

"Is Harper here? I saw her car outside."

"She's doing some outdoor chores for me," Rose said. "Sticks don't pick up themselves, and my back isn't what it used to be."

"I see." Jo frowned, not sure how to start. She didn't want to sound like she was accusing Rose's great-niece of anything, but she also didn't want the older woman to be taken advantage of.

"I can see something is on your mind, Jo. You might as well just spit it out."

Jo took a deep breath. "Well, right after the funeral, we ran into Harper, and Nick thought he recognized her. She said they hadn't met, though."

Rose looked at her blankly. "I see."

"Well, he was certain that he was right about having met her, so he did some thinking and realized she gave him and his sister a tour of a nursing home a few months ago."

"That makes sense," Rose said. "She used to work at one out in Port Austin."

"So, you know that she was fired, then?" Jo asked, relaxing slightly.

Rose frowned. "Fired? No, that's not right. She quit – she wanted to have more time to spend helping me. I told her she shouldn't put her life on hold for me, but she said she was happy to do it."

"I'm not saying she was lying about her motivations for coming out here to help you, but Nick told me that he called the nursing home she worked at, and they told him that she'd been fired. He said that she had been accused of stealing medication from some of the residents."

Rose's brows drew together. "No, that doesn't sound right. I remember she told me when she gave her two weeks' notice. They must be mistaken."

"Maybe," Jo said. She bit her lip, not sure what to do next. Either Harper or the nursing home was lying, and she didn't think it was the nursing home.

"We can ask her," Rose said, making as if to rise out of her chair.

"It's all right," Jo said quickly. "I don't think it's that important." She didn't want Harper to know that she had been gossiping about her, even if what she was saying was true.

"Really, we can just ask," Rose said. "It won't be a problem."

Jo opened her mouth to say it really wasn't necessary, but at that moment it seemed fate decided for her. The front door opened, and Harper stepped in. She gave Jo a friendly smile and then stepped to the side, a man coming in behind her. It was Dale, the farmer Jo had spoken to just a few days ago. He tipped his hat to her, then turned to Rose.

"Nice day, ma'am."

"Hello, Dale," Rose said. "What can we do for you?"

"Sorry for dropping by unexpectedly, but I was wondering if you've given any more thought to my offer."

"I'm not selling any of my land until I'm cold and buried," Rose said. "If you want to lease some, though, we can talk about that."

Dale shook his head, looking irritated. "I told you, I'm not paying for improvements to land I'm leasing. It's all or nothing, Rose."

Rose just shrugged. "Then, it's going to be nothing. I've given you my terms, and I'm not going to change my mind. I've had a lot of time to practice being stubborn."

He sighed. "I guess I'll just have to take your answer as it is." He slid his gaze over to Jo, who immediately put her hands up.

"Oh, no, don't look at me like that. I'm not selling off any land, either."

He gave a resigned chuckle. "All right, all right. I get the message loud and clear. You both appreciate what you've got."

"Well, now that that's out of the way, we might as well make the best of this little gathering. I made some chocolate chip cookies earlier today. If one of you wants to go get them out of the kitchen, we can have some while we chat. Just because neither of us are going to sell you our land, Dale, doesn't mean we can't all be friends."

"I agree," he said easily. "No hard feelings. I'll grab those cookies. Consider it my apology for nagging you about the parcel of land."

He moved away to the kitchen. Once he was gone, Rose beckoned Harper over, giving Jo a meaningful look. Realizing that the older woman was going to ask Harper about the nursing home, Jo excused herself.

"I'll go help with the cookies," she muttered as she rose.

She hurried into the kitchen, coming to a stop when she saw Dale. His back was to her, and he was stirring a glass of milk. On the counter next to him was a tiny plastic bottle like she saw the morning of Andrea's death.

Filled with a sudden sense of uneasiness, she took a step back, only to freeze when her shoes squeaked on the floor and the clinking sound of the spoon going around and around in the glass halted as Dale froze.

CHAPTER THIRTEEN

He turned his head to look at her, his brows drawing together when he saw who it was. Then, he turned fully, his body blocking the glass of milk and the little plastic bottle.

"Did Rose want something?" he asked.

"No," Jo said, her voice lacking the confidence she usually had. She told herself she was being ridiculous. Dale had no reason to want to kill Andrea. Except… maybe he hadn't been trying to kill her. What if Rose was the real target all along? Rose, whose land Dale wanted so badly. Feeling her heart begin to pound as the realization that Dale very well could be a murderer came over her, she quickly added, "She wanted to talk with Harper for a moment, so I excused myself and came in here. Do you need any help with the cookies?"

He nodded at the platter, which was sitting on the island. "Go ahead and take those in. I'm pouring glasses of milk for everyone. I'll be right out."

She nodded, taking the cookies, and heading back toward Rose's living room. Harper had gone, and Rose was gazing off into the distance. She looked up when Jo put the plate of cookies on the table. "Well, that didn't go well."

"I'm sorry for causing trouble," Jo said. "I shouldn't have mentioned anything. It's not my business."

"No, I'm glad you did." She sighed. "It turned out she did lie to me. She was fired from the nursing home and was too embarrassed over the whole thing to tell me about it. She wasn't behind the drug thefts, though. She showed me an email they sent her apologizing and telling her the real person responsible had been caught."

"I can understand why she was embarrassed. If that sort of rumor got out around town, it might keep her from getting hired anywhere else, even if it wasn't true."

"Still, she shouldn't have lied to me," Rose said with disappointment, shaking her head. "Don't worry, though, Jo, she won't be mad at you for telling me. Not for too long, anyway. She knows you're just watching out for me."

"I still feel bad," Jo muttered as Dale came to the room. He was carrying four glasses of milk awkwardly and paused to look around for Harper.

"It will just be the three of us," Rose said. "Oh, milk, what a good idea."

He carefully set one of the glasses down in front of Rose and put the others on the table between him and Jo. Jo frowned at the milk, still not sure what she had seen. Milk didn't need to be stirred. She was certain he had been mixing something into it. But what if it was medicine for himself? Maybe he was lactose intolerant – she was pretty sure there was a powder people with that condition could mix into dairy to make it safe to consume.

Still, she couldn't take any chances with Rose's life. She reached for Rose's glass of milk, figuring she could pretend to drink it, and Rose could have a different glass. If Dale hadn't done anything to it, he shouldn't mind.

She reached for the milk, but before she could touch the glass, his hand reached out and moved it away from her. He gave her a strange look. "That's for Rose."

"They're all the same," she said.

"Then why don't you take one of these?" He gestured at the other glasses on the coffee table. "They're closer to you."

She held his gaze, unsure of what to do. Oblivious to what was going on, Rose reached for the glass. She lifted it to her lips and Jo lashed out, knocking it from her hands. It flew through the air, spinning around and throwing milk everywhere before falling to the carpet. Rose was frozen in shock, covered in spilled milk.

"Why did you do that?" she gasped.

"He put something in the milk," Jo said. "I saw him stirring it — and he had a little bottle of eyedrops next to it, like the one I found that morning."

"Eyedrops?" Rose asked, confused. Jo didn't understand that either, but from Dale's slowly reddening face, she guessed she was on the right track.

"Have you lost your mind?" he asked.

"I saw you stirring the milk," she repeated stubbornly. "If you didn't add anything to it, then what were you doing?"

He hesitated and Rose leaned back slowly, comprehension dawning on her face.

"I left you alone in the kitchen with the freshly made lemonade the morning Andrea died," she said, narrowing her eyes. "Is what Jo is saying true? Did you really poison the lemonade?"

"You're both insane," he said, standing up. "I don't have to take this."

"Hold on," Jo said rising. "You can't just go. We – we have to call the police…" She trailed off, not sure how this went. She had never actually called the police on someone before. When he turned to give her a dark look, she quelled, realizing that maybe she shouldn't have mentioned calling the police until he was gone.

"No police," he said. "I didn't do anything and you're just going to have to take my word for it. Are we clear?"

"Definitely not," Jo said, trying to get some of her courage back. "I don't know what's going on, but there's obviously something that you don't want the police to look into, and that means it's something bad. And – I think you just tried to poison Rose. I'm not going to let you get away with that."

"Don't forget, I know where you sleep," he said in a low voice. "I know just how little security you have on your farm."

"Are you threatening me?" Jo asked, her voice getting high.

"You're threatening my freedom. I think it's fair."

"Oh, dear," Rose said faintly from behind her. Jo turned to see the older woman pressing a hand to her chest and slowly sink back into her chair. "I'm not feeling so well. The stress – I don't know if I can handle it."

Jo tried to move toward her, but Dale caught her wrist. "You're not going anywhere," he muttered.

"But Rose… I have to help her."

"Not going to happen." He yanked her away, toward the kitchen. Jo turned, desperate to get back to Rose, who looked like she was about to faint. Dale was too strong, though – he had been a farmer his whole life, and Jo didn't have a chance of pulling out of his grip.

"What are you doing?" she snapped when he finally let go of her in the kitchen – with his large body between her and the door.

"Letting nature take its course," he replied. "If she has a heart attack, that solves most of my problems. I'm sorry, Jo, but I can't let you leave, either. You should've just kept quiet. I like you well enough – you've got a good head on your shoulders, and my wife will be sad to hear about your unfortunate accident."

"What accident?" she asked, her heart feeling like it was pounding in her throat.

He reached into his pocket and pulled out a little bottle of eyedrops. She squinted at the label, and yes, that was what it was. It was hard to feel threatened by eyedrops.

"An accident with eyedrops?"

"These eyedrops have an ingredient meant to reduce the red in your eyes. That chemical is called tetrahydrozoline. I learned about it from one of those murder shows my wife likes to watch on TV in the evening. If consumed, it can be toxic, especially in larger doses. It also doesn't have a strong taste or smell, so it's very easy to slip into drinks unnoticed. Symptoms are depressed breathing, headaches, trembling, dizziness, and eventually a coma or death if not caught." He turned the bottle to read the label, shaking his head. "It should have been the perfect crime. I figured no one would look too closely at a woman her age dropping dead suddenly. The symptoms are rather similar to that of a stroke or heart attack. I need that land, Jo. I thought after her husband passed, I would be able to buy at least some of it, but she won't let go of so much as an acre. I never planned for anyone other than her to get hurt, of course, and I do regret this."

"You could've killed anyone with the lemonade," Jo gasped. "How did you know that Harper wouldn't drink it, or me? What if she'd had your wife over for pie, for goodness' sake?"

"I had to take the risk that there might be collateral damage, and my wife was busy with her family that day," he said. "I can't see my farm go under like so many others have. Like I said, I'm sorry you got caught in it, but there's no going back now."

"You can't make me drink that," she said, crossing her arms. "I know you're stronger than me, but I'm pretty sure it's still not going to be easy for you to force eyedrops down my throat. I'll just spit them back out."

He reached under his jacket and pulled out an old revolver, aiming it at her. With one hand he tossed her the eyedrops, which she didn't reach out to catch. The bottle fell to the floor, but unfortunately didn't spill open. He cocked the hammer back, a familiar sound, and not one she had ever had a reason to fear before.

"You can drink them, or you can get shot. If I were you, I'd drink them. You'll have a little bit of time before it starts to take effect – who knows, you might get lucky between now and then. At the very least, I'll let you write out a will. I won't show it to anyone, but I'll make sure your livestock gets sold off to whoever you want them to go to."

Her hands shaking, she bent down to pick up the

container of eyedrops. He was right – she would choose a delayed death over an instant one.

Frightened, she lifted the bottle to her lips. Before she touched her lips to it, she heard the louder sound of a shotgun being racked. Dale jumped and turned around to find Rose standing in the kitchen doorway, aiming an old pump action shotgun at his chest. Jo felt a rush of relief and stepped to the side, so she was out of the line of fire, then quickly tossed the bottle of eyedrops away. She would never be able to look at them the same way again and really hoped she didn't develop dry eyes in her future.

"I suggest you drop it," Rose said. "This is a twelve gauge, and it's loaded with buckshot. From this distance, it's going to do a lot more damage than whatever you've got in that little pea shooter of yours, and I'm willing to take my chances that you'll miss. Are you willing to do the same?"

With a look of barely constrained anger on his face, he carefully lowered his revolver to the floor and raised his hands. In the other room, Jo could hear Harper on the phone, talking to the police. Her heart still had the dregs of adrenaline racing through her system. She hurried away from Dale and went to stand next to Rose. Still worried for the older woman's health, she whispered, "Are you okay?"

Rose winked at her, keeping the shotgun trained on Dale. "Sometimes, it pays to be old. No one accuses a little old lady of faking a heart attack. Apparently, the trick even works on murderers."

EPILOGUE

Jo leaned against the fence, watching the two baby alpacas playing in the field. The one who had been born first, the fawn girl, she had decided to name Bean, after vanilla beans. The little white one, a male, still didn't have a name, as he had been born only a few days ago. He had found his feet quickly and now the two of them romped through the field together, playing almost like puppies.

Jo smiled. The alpacas didn't know or care about what had taken place at Rose's house several days ago and didn't carry the same weights that she did. Jo wasn't sure how to feel. She knew that she, Harper, and Rose were lucky to have gotten out of the situation alive. But Andrea hadn't been as lucky, so it felt wrong to be too glad of her own safety. At the same time, she couldn't help the feeling that her trust in people had been broken just a little. If someone as seemingly normal as Dale could resort to murder, then what could she rely on? Everything seemed different.

There was also the fact that Cole still wasn't talking to her, and that didn't seem to be changing anytime soon. If she was being honest with herself, she didn't know how to feel about their breakup. She didn't think he was entirely wrong. Now that she had some distance from it, she could accept that they were two different people. At the same time, she wished that he would listen to her and believe her that nothing had been going on with Nick. If Cole wanted to break up with her for who she was, she would have to accept that, but she didn't have to let him go on believing that she had done something to break his trust.

She felt as if, over the past few weeks, her life had taken a sudden turn for the unexpected and had yet to get back on track. With Cole out of her life, Nick back in it, a neighbor sent to prison for murder, and far more knowledge about how deadly simple medications could be than she had ever wanted to know, a return to normal seemed impossible. Maybe she should take the example of the alpacas to heart and just be happy with the present moment – the world was always changing, but as long as the alpacas had food to eat, good company, and plenty of space to romp around in, they were happy. Jo had all of that and more. The sun was going to shine, and the birds were going to chirp, whether she was enjoying them or not, and it seemed a waste to let herself be miserable on such a nice day.

Printed in Great Britain
by Amazon